the giver in me honors the giver in you.
xo. adrian michael

giver.

giver.
I

adrian michael

a lovasté project
in partnership with hwttbtw
published by
creative genius
CONCORDHAUS

lovaste.com

Copyright © 2020 by Adrian Michael Green

Published by Creative Genius Publishing—
an imprint of lovasté

| Denver, CO | Concord, CA |

To contact the author visit adrianmichaelgreen.com
To see more of the author's work visit IG @adrianmichaelgreen
Book jacket designed by Adrian Michael Green

ISBN-13: 9798608300578

Printed in the United States of America

for the givers.

the year of the giver.

remember the time you cared so much it became to be too much for them to handle. and you tried to pull back and pull back and pull back just enough so that your caring and your hearting and your showing was downplayed for their benefit. for their comfort. for their ease. and for what. so they didn't have to try to match your effort. so they didn't have to tip into a zone they weren't familiar with. as you do)because you are you(you adjusted. and you cared. to provide them a version of someone they could stand. they could be on the same frequency with. but not anymore. no longer is this the time to play small. to downplay. to hinder. now you don't apologize for how much care you are willing to express. it's on them to meet you where you are. not because you are inconsiderate. but because this is the season of the giver. the season of the wanderer. the season of the lover. the season of the heart. reclaim your super power and realize how necessary you have always been.

critical self talk.

love yourself. love your worth.

stop looking for love.

stop looking for love
in temporary places
in temporary humans
because
your kind of love
is a forever kind
kind of like
never ever ending
always
but you keep giving
and giving and giving
your forever love
to temporary people
who can't seem to
meet you at that level
so stop looking
)not loving(
)never stop your forever love(
for love
in those placeholders
and it all will
come back to you
by you
for you

you don't belong in a cage.

you don't belong in a cage. tho many would want to see you stay put and fight yourself within the bars. but your wings are too big and your beak is too strong and your will is too fierce to stay put and stay contained and stay behind bars that others would want you to remain. no dear giver do what feels best. break and bend and sear and bust any and every barrior to your success. to your happiness. to your desire that transcends all desires. you don't belong in a cage. you belong in the wild. you belong in a world that smiles back and bends like the wind instead of bouncing back making it feel like you don't belong. but you do belong. anywhere and everywhere. my god my goddess my universe you have so much in you that no wonder they want you controlled so they can reap off your back and off your mind and off your soul to do their bidding to do their work to do their ease. but you don't belong in their cage. not how they see you. not how they want you to be. you are a creature with no master a soul with no captain. you are your own guide and your own fortune. and that inspires other birds other spirits other beings to break free. cage free.

leaving is for saving yourself.

don't leave them without loving them.
say to them you love them too deeply
to stay if you must leave.
say to them you love them too intensely
to watch them not try anymore.
say to them you love them
and walk away
they may find you another day
but leaving isn't for their sake
leaving is for saving yourself
from being drained
again.

don't remove yourself from your own universe.

i know you sometimes want to take the moon out of your sky. and dim your sun. and pull down your stars and just fade. just fade. just. fade. because too many someone's told you you're too big. too bold. too hot. too loud. too vibrant. but stay all those things. stay and don't remove yourself from your own universe. let them eat their words everytime they see you.

love is a runway.

love is a runway. you are either running towards it.
or running away from it. the very act of running isn't simply
moving fast as it is moving at a pace that seemingly feels fast. too
fast for some. too slow for others. but the run itself is sprint nor
marathon. the run itself is a choice. conscious effort to move in a
direction. all ways create feelings. all directions create something
that bubbles up in self or in others. what matters most is knowing
your purpose. knowing your why. and always asking: am i running
away or running towards. either way you're on your way back. the
question is are you taking the scenic route.

you don't need to be saved.

you don't need to be saved or have someone hero you. you are your own hero saving yourself looking for another hero saving their own life. together maybe on your own heroes journey. to give one another. to love one another. on the same frequency. no more. no less. balanced. but balance doesn't always mean equal. it means pulling weight. holding the task you both decide. to carry one another. to pour into one another. to run with not run over. spilling. spilling. spilling. and not apologizing or have to look over your shoulder once you are empty and need reloading.

wildchild.

wildchild. blanketed in vulnerability. wildchild. moving to new
towns. wildchild. making new and amazing relationships.
wildchild. cultivating and securing boundaries. wildchild. taking
trips as the moon tides the sea to beach. wildchild. dancing with
rain before it evaporates on your skin. wildchild. music sings for
you. wildchild. trusting your own divinity. wildchild. going places.
wildchild. evereverblooming. wildchild. loving loving friend.
wildchild. human wrapped in soul. lover with no end.

you're the kind of smoke that causes fires.

you're the kind of smoke that causes fires.

you are an earthshaking love.

you are an earthshaking love.

fights we make.

love doesn't mean staying. it means give to the unknown and accept what comes. to stay and to go are both fights we make. different battles. same war.

sunsets.

like sunsets you provide color and have undeniable beauty.
you don't take breaths you give breaths. reminding souls to
breathe in with the wind and breathe out with the waves. your
dock sits where it must. amongst the crashing. holding whatever
tries to weigh you down.

grace and soul that pours from you.

without trying there is much grace and soul that pours from you.
humans who just provide this love deserve utmost kindness and
care. but like you there is no need for the give to echo back.

the roses you bloom.

you deserve roses upon roses from the roses you bloom
for yourself. and you shouldn't have to ask to be flowered.
all the water you give the sun would nourish the world.

favorite position.

your favorite position is being misunderstood. being underdog.
being on top as they watch in shock. the wings on your back will
only get you to higher heights. but you have to believe heights
don't exist before you vanquish them.

their traumas aren't yours.

their traumas aren't yours.
don't let them trigger you.
but if they do
give them back
not the wound
not the blood
not the shovel
pour sugar
down
down
deep
deep
in
in
and
don't beg
to trade
trauma for trauma
but
trade
love for love
sometimes
love
you have to be the one
who fights back with your love
walking away in the opposite direction

eye language.

your eyes have a language of their own.
few can decipher but you aren't in need
to be unlocked. but whoever reaches
your frequency your elevation your plane
won't need a key.

the deepest heart.

best part of you is your heart. anyone who comes around can't think clearly but feel deeply.

the movement you are.

movements like you catch fire. and blaze trails. and there are times
you can't see your flames. your blaze. your heat. but i can. the
tiniest pinhole into your soul is enough for me to know that all
the wonders of the world seek you. awe you. love you. turn to you.
for guidance. for inspiration. and people like you melt us quickly.
and love us with that same intensity. what a movement you are. a
revolution.

sweet honey.

honey is sweet and it cures and there is no doubt you're mixed
with these powers to heal. the power to pull. the power to influ-
ence. just by putting your mind on the one you love. that is what
seperates you. your thought. your detail. your kindess. going out
of the way. the extra mile. the reaching. the care. the sweetest love.
sweet honey love you spill down the throats with your words your
acts your heart.

taking isn't in your vocabulary.

taking isn't in your vocabulary.

the flaws you have.

the flaws you have make you the most beautiful human. they don't stop you from living and loving. you are mature enough and wise enough and aware enough to see what is meant to destroy you. to be what is part of you. to acknowledge and water and celebrate as part of your garden. weeds have purpose, too.

let go and let universe.

givers
let go
and let
universe
and
accept
what
may
come
by
not
blocking
their
own
path.

learn to accept.

how much love you give and how much you take is in your control. and the way your soul is set up, receiving can be a challenge.
gifts. compliments. love. sometimes those with the biggest hearts
can't easily accept the role of recipient.

time to cleanse your space.

when fall comes, depart from what it is you don't need. time to cleanse from spaces that undervalue you or you've outgrown. this isn't negative or too much to ask. you have to do what is in your best interest. not everyone should have easy access to your energy. protect your giving.

bloom into your own kind of beautiful.

you have transformed and bloomed into your own kind of
beautiful. many will try to diminish or downplay your growth.
pay them no attention. enjoy your season.

you are the one.

you are the one
who is capable enough
strong enough
soft enough
to love yourself
better than
anyone else.

beauty has no reason to rush.

trust your heart
listen when it feels
you'll know what to do
you always do
and if it takes some time
take that time
beauty has no reason to rush.

return to self.

let nature heal you.
grow in peace.
then begin again.

you are a constant
work in process.

a givers daily mantra.

deep.
dope.
deliberate.

how to stay whole.

begging for acceptance
teaches how to break in half.
loving who you are
teaches you how to stay whole.

begging to be seen or validated will drain you. it will take a lot of
energy away from your true authentic self that at some point you
may not even recognize who you are; given that you change and
morph into what you hope others would appreciate. notice if you
do this. exert attention onto yourself. love yourself. give yourself
the attention that you beg from others and become who you are
meant to be.

be on watch.

watch for wolves
they sometimes
look like sheep.

stay open.

be open. especially in moments you just want to be closed. that's power in your control. and stay alert. some would pounce to take advantage. but just because you're open doesn't mean you're a fool.

let them be rocks. you be water.

let them be rocks. you be water.

break old habits.

to truly heal break old habits. close doors that have been open way too long. notice when what you give is being used against you. walk away from toxic situations and watch your whole aura change.

soak yourself in love.

soak yourself in love. this is not for others. this is for you. you need to give yourself what you pour and spill into others. self love is self care. always pay attention to yourself.

love is a light. a purpose.

love is a light. a purpose. when you find it it will never go out.

overflow.

give yourself permission to change
and try things that will help you overflow.

stay you. always.

courage is being yourself and never apologizing for it.
stay you. always.

your heart is too damn big.

your heart is too damn big to be tucked away
and hidden in someone's back pocket.

dusk and dawn.

what you manifest comes true. because you are a true vision. and
visionaries see things that others overlook. but you aren't like
that. seers look beyond what can be seen not with the eyes but
with soul. and that takes more than empathy and more than trust.
you need both of those but the most necessary ingredient is you.
how you bring such elegance and ease and appeal. so much so
the clouds part as you begin to show the weather. one glance and
everyone is in a standstill. waiting. waiting. waiting. for your next
arrival. you are the thin line between dusk and dawn.

blessed to love. blessed to feel.

blessed to love and blessed to feel. you'd have it no other way. it isn't a curse and it isn't something you complain about. because speaking ill about love and feeling is speaking ill of you and that shatters your own heart which doesn't need any more breaking. any more negativity. any more pain. there was a time you'd make space for bad energy to consume you because someone made it a habit to bring you down in order for you to second guess your worth your heart your being. but those days are long gone and you see yourself as a blessing. cursing only conjures an old pattern not worth revisiting in the present.

darkness and light.

many think that darkness is jealous of light. that the two have a deep tension. but light and dark need each other because both get to see you in different hues. they compare notes just to see what the other didn't get the chance to experience. their envy is only in missing what the other gets to glimpse. it is in the sharing that makes them feel closest to you.

the focused muse.

some may see you as mean or hard to read. a mystery. but they
will never understand what it looks like when someone who has
their eye on something far greater. and nothing or no one can
stand in their way. you aren't mean. you're focused. with the will
of a lion and the sprint of a gazelle. preparing for your time in
the sun. but don't feel pressured to always explain yourself. stay
in your zone. if they really love you they will not need assurance.
just one look in your eye and they will see such beautiful
determination.

buried seeds grow deep.

flowers grow in even the harshest circumstance. it is the seed
from which you rise. and despite any hard condition, the flower
will come alive. this is you, dear flower, abundant no matter the
season. you grow and you sprout and you blossom any and everywhere. and sometimes people underestimate the power of a seed.
they will try to bury you in soil that has been told to be pillaged
and void of life but they don't know how resilient and strong and
courageous you are. being planted and being buried are two different things. you plant yourself. others try to bury and hide you. but
buried seeds grow deep. and your roots are impeccable. so if they
uproot you and try to bury your soul they will have no luck. bury-
ing you is the best thing they could ever do because once planted
all those seeds inside you will frontfire and fertilize all that once
was thought to be lost and new life will breathe your air.

out of reach.

you are out of reach. not because you are too good.
because you are searching for what doesn't exist yet.
and when you latch onto what you seek
holding it will be bittersweet.

raw emotion is your super power.

raw emotion is your super power.

obstacles.

any obstacle in your way is just a test. you'll get by it by going
through it and the dust behind you will quickly settle so that those
that come after you see the hustle and heartwork it takes to be
as dope as you. not to brag or boast but sometimes you need to
express some elevated confidence so they know you're the best.

sunflower twin flame.

the sunflower next to your skin is simply your twin flame telling
you how nice it is to see you again.

999,998.00

your worth multiplies each time you speak positively. when words leave your lips the words breeze across your face just to remind you of what you said. and then and then it reaches the sun who whispers to the moon and stars just to gossip about you. did you know the universe places bets that you will inspire millions of souls. right now you're at 999,998.00

find and create yourself.

find and create yourself.

sadness into sunshine.

you can't be broken. even at your worst what seems to break already begins to reform. there is always something magical and powerful about someone who turns sadness into sunshine.

command and conquer.

look back
look back
to see
how far
you've come
then
look forward
look forward
to see
what
you're
about
to
command
and
conquer.

thermometer.

your smile changes the entire temperature in a room.
even if they try they can't hide how much you make them
sweat.

a rose and its thorns.

it isn't your petals that need loving. it is your thorns.
if they can stand to be pricked they can stand the test of time.
petals are too easy to be appreciated. it is always the sharp edges
the parts of us that cut without warning, that indicate who,
if anyone, can handle a rose and its thorns.

infinite possibilities.

you are endless. you are infinite possibilities.
and that is rare beauty in human form.

bold and brave.

you are perseverance and lightning in a bottle. no matter what happens you have this way about you that lasts and fights and takes the blows with your head held high. there is a beast inside you that growls when unwarranted souls near you or those you love dearly. protective and peaceful you aren't to be messed with. and that is what people love about you. you grit and you claw and you love and you war. you are bold. you are brave.

the great pyramids.

there is a foundation that must be built before a pyramid can
amass eminence. your values and your compass guide you when
the winds get high and life attempts to jolt you. but challenge is
your appetite. and you are laying the final bricks and ready
for the next tier.

become the storm.

you look best next to bright colors. just right underneath the sky
beside a field of nature's glory. when you return there you get
recharged there no wonder earth tones compliment you so well.
but sometimes you don't feel so bright and you avoid going outside. the wild you've abandoned you lose who you are. and that
is normal. sometimes we lose and forget and avoid from time to
time. but this world and every soul in it becomes colorless when
you step away. when you retreat. when you feel like the pressure of
being you gets the best of you. you're human. we all have doubts
and want to shut dark clouds out. but when you face the storm the
storm subsides once you face it once you face it once you face it.
for when difficulty comes and stares you in your eyes it crumbles
because you won't back down. you won't surrender. you won't dare
call it quits. you give too much of yourself and that is why you
feel depleted and have nothing left for yourself. that is the biggest
storm biggest crisis biggest obstacle. but when you become the
storm there is no storm left.

dream catcher.

you are a dream catcher. a fulfilling fantasy. imagination comes
to you and requests advice on how to proceed. people come to
you with their life plan. with their aspirations. with their worries.
with their insecurities. your ability to listen and ask questions is
the very cypher that gives them hope and understanding. you are
the bridge to happiness. all roads lead to you. don't forget to catch
your own dreams. don't forget your way home.

crown.

your crown is not a physical item. it can't be seen with the naked eye. your crown is lodged under under. underground. people will dig for it. claw for it. dirty their fingers trying to grasp for it. but no one can touch it. no one can touch it. the crown was never meant to be worn on your head. the crown is the glow of your soul. the shimmer of stardust in your bones. the energy you pass to another. the gasp between each breath. your crown is priceless. your crown is your greatest inheritance worth more once you realize the crown was never meant to be kept it's always meant to be given. passed around.

when a butterfly gets its wings.

vintage instant classic.
you facing the fall.
there is nothing more astounding
when a butterfly gets its wings.

you can't judge a soul.

you can't judge a soul by looks alone
or looks at all. you must never judge
simply observe. notice the curve of
their desires and the content of their
character. there you will find
another window another door
to simply notice and observe.

rebel souls.

rebel souls have a way of doing their own thing while others push for them to conform. rebel souls resist status quo not because it's cool or a fad but because deep within them there is a need for truth and doing the right thing. rebel souls define counter culture and re-define what it means to oppose. they are spotlights in blindspots to rage against the machine.

falling deep deep deeply.

falling deep deep deeply is how you love.

naked nude.

you give how they want it. you are considerate and flow in ways
that others need. this doesn't mean you change who you are. this
means you have mastered your current. your ways. your abilities.
to monitor the requests on how much of you they require. and in
your wake you siphon pieces you're willing to let go. all of you if
you wanted. but sometimes you have to keep most of yourself so
you have some of you left.

the sun and her curves.

the sun and her curves hold no candle to you. the heat you radiate burns in such a way that the sun contemplates you. seeks you. looks to you. you see. even the brightest star turns to you.

no pain. no power.

when you are all in then pain is bound to happen. pain is part
of the process. pain can be intolerable especially when doing
something or around someone that isn't worth waiting to see on
the other side of hardship. but pain sharpens and strengthens
your power. your tenacity. your toughness. when times get rough
and when you want to up and leave. pain is a sign of tension to
tease out and maintain. pain is discomfort. uncomfortable feelings
that tells you something may be wrong. as it throbs and stabs and
aches and pinches you're steady. you're steady. you're steady. as if
pain doesn't faze you. but you have been there. you speak the language of pain. not because you have a high tolerance. but because
you know how to manage mild and severe situations without
adding to the pain itself.

you are bottled up poetry.

you are bottled up poetry. the way you intoxicate and linger.
flavorful with hints of sass and sexiness one glass is never enough.
your label simple and elegant. unknown inside. but the pour of
you sends epic chills you are a rare fine wine.

dpc.

you deserve to be loved how you love:
deeply. passionately. completely.
those who can't give this want to give this.
want to be this. for you. with you. they don't
want to lose you. be away from you. why
would they. they have the best thing. best
soul. best gem of them all. but they are close
)way too close(to rupturing this. their lungs
just aren't strong enough to stay under.
but you provide hope and care to show them
how to breathe. how to take in water.
how to sway and bob and imitate you.
but they can't be you. they can't.
and that is hard for you. to find yourself.
because no one ever complained
about the love you give.

more than human.

you are fascinating. there is this kind of sparkle in your eye.
the kind you get while crossing a bridge. and the horizon itself
meets all surrounding nature and urban elements. you blend
the two worlds. you collide them. you are the bridge itself.
to a place people can only imagine to visit. you are this in
real-time. in real life. in real skin. you are more than human.
more than a dream. more than skin. more than what anyone
could ever try and box you in. you escape line and angle.
you are what the egyptians used to plan masterpieces.

regret.

they will regret passing you up.
and you will thank them. you will
forget you had a thing for them. a
thought for them. a future wasn't
written. what a gift. to know you
now have the chance to be your
fullness. your entire moon phase
without needing to shape shift.
heart shift. you don't have to
break yourself or constrain
who you are just to fit in.
fit out. fit out. fit out.
for it is them who
will find their
loss was
your
gain.

everything everything.

you are remarkable. phenomenal. outstanding. stunning. you're
worth staying up late to watch the sun set and waking up early to
see rise. you are full of wonder. it's unfortunate if the one you're
chasing doesn't vibe with you or notice how brilliant you are.
because everything about you is admirable. everything everything.
from the quirks that would bother to the thoughts that leave your
lips. from your body)that lovely body(to your soul that gets to
bounce around up against your skin)that beautiful skin(it's such
bizarre news to know that not everyone sees you. sees majesty
to be adored. you are everything everything. remember this
always. remind yourself always. whatever you want to be. you are.
whatever has your attention is blessed to be held even if
momentarily. this is not hyperbole this is fact. this is no exaggera-
tion. no one is you. but they want to be you. because you are
everything everything. and the beautiful thing about you is you
don't see this or say this or draw this about you. the giver in you
won't allow it. but for a time right now just take this in. hold yourself to this page and feel all the things your soul has always known.

the space between.

you are so loved.
you are so abundantly loved.
and at times you may not feel like you are.
and at times you think no one loves you.
you're human. you're human.
you can have days that question you.
days that feel like crates on your chest.
moments that wipe you out.
and at times you think you can't escape it.
and at times you wish you had someone.
someone to understand without question.
someone to hold you without fixing you.
someone to get it without you saying anything.
you are the space between the space between.
eager to know a love that lasts. a love that resonates.
a love that fills all the buckets. this love is yours.
all of it. what drips from you returns to you.
you are the love you seek.

your sun is coming .

the one you want may not be the one for you. and that's hard.
brutal even. because you will try to make it work. you can't force
the sun to rise. it just happens. your sun is coming. and when it
does it will be epic.

all-in kind of love.

you deserve an all-in kind of love.
the kind that has your back when
people try to drag your name in the mud.
the kind that shows up when you tell them
you just want to be alone.
the kind that doesn't need to be validated.
the kind that stays. that lasts. that lasts.

you were always enough.

you were always enough.
your enough was just too
much for them.

my hope for you.

may the one
you fall in love with
really see you
not the idea of you
the real you
and never try
to turn you into who
they want you to be.

they will find you.

they will find you
when you least expect
and you'll think they are
just like the rest
but they won't
tear down your walls
or only want
that thing
they will be everything
you imagined.

stay close to people that feel like home.

stay close to people
that feel like home.

sometimes you feel like not giving.

when you reach out
and don't find their hand
pull yours back
they will then know
how it feels to starve
for a love that gives nothing
in return.

your heart will beat over 100,000 times today.

your heart will beat over 100,000 times today.
don't waste any of its energy on people and things
that will try and break it. protect your heart.
and this can be hard. reserving your love.
because you just want to pour. you just want to pour.
every hour on the hour before the hour even ends.
to anyone and everyone. that's who you are.
unlike any other. people tell you to pull back
not because they care to see where it goes
but because they want it all to themselves.
this is different. this is so you don't love on empty.
a well can only hold so much water without sinking itself.
don't sink to a point where you can't bring yourself back.
don't feel bad if you choose to preserve a bit for you.
wasting for those undeserving shouldn't be given
any attention from you.

giving mentality.

strong relationships exist when two people
acknowledge their struggles. actively work
on them. and love on each other especially
in moments when it hurts. this is your gift.
to struggle with and trench and mud. you
give and give and give and give and give
but you can't be strong by yourself doing
overtime. they need to step up or step aside.

swim in your feelings.

it's okay to be all up in your feelings.
swim in them. lay under them like you're
moon bathing. the more you spend with
your heart, the better you understand
and love yourself.

no wonder everyone falls for you.

that sunlight you shine blooms hearts.
no wonder everyone falls for you.

the deepest ocean.

your half smile doesn't mean sadness. tho to some it peaks of
melancholy hues. but no, your mouth is a gatekeeper that says,
you think you know me but you only see the snow at the top of my
underwater mountain. i'm the deepest ocean you have ever seen.
but i'm not sure i even want to let you in to swim.

madly in love.

find someone who makes
you feel madly in love.

soulflower rose.

a flower never
needs a mirror
to know where
it's petals are
or how colorful
it has bloomed.

peace of the rain.

you can be sunshine
and still have cloudy skies
let love light your day
even when it rains.

hard days come and hard days go but it seems the hardest last
longest. so take little reminders whatever those are)words, people,
items(and touch them during those darkest hours. physically they
may not be there or they're just out of reach, so be what you need.
say and think them into existence. collect yourself how best you
can. but do not rush the missing part, or the grieving part, or the
hurting part, or the feeling part. rest in your sadness if just for a
little while. there you will find healing. there you'll find peace.

sometimes it is hard to get up.

sometimes it is hard to get up. but when you gather enough courage to stand and face fear or doubt or anxiety, you get better at taking all those things that try and stop you with you.

respect and boundaries.

family is everything. but never let someone talk down to you. curse you. or call you out of your name because they think they can. create boundaries. and if it continues to happen, distance yourself or cut ties completely. you deserve to be respected.

deuces.

you shouldn't have to beg
for love and affection. no more
trying so hard to get their attention.
or begging to be loved. being you is
enough and if they can't see it or make
you adjust who you are to fit their skewed
fantasy then give them the deuces.

love you more.

give yourself
the gift of love.

baby you deserve.

you deserve someone who seeks comfort
inside your beautiful sacred relationship.

you deserve to rest peacefully at night
without wondering if they still care.

you deserve a lover who: cooks for you.
cleans for you. takes you out. opens your door.
holds your hand. tells you how they feel.

you deserve effort and sacrifice. not excuses
and selfishness. half love isn't love.

you deserve to crash into someone who loves you
and everything that you're insecure about.

you deserve to be someone's first choice.

you deserve to be happy and a love that never evaporates.

you deserve kind words. selfless acts. romance.
deep connection. chemistry. attention. desire.

you deserve a lover who is completely devoted to you.

you deserve someone who tells you they miss you. your flaws.
the void you cause when gone.

you give and give with no desire for anything in return. you
deserve that kind of big love from someone other than yourself.

exist loudly and love deeply.

you're the kind of human that inspires others
to exist loudly and love deeply.

fierce and gentle.

you can be firece and gentle. lightning and rain.
your attitude is always beautiful. and there are many times they
can't handle the wind that goes with your wings. the singe that
comes with your fire. you don't mean to be so direct but that is
what you bring to situations rather than avoiding or hiding or
pretending everything is okay. it is important to be real. you are
real. and you want everyone around you to be real. that is what
you want. that is what you give. the clang of your tongue is only as
sharp as the truth that comes from it. and your truth feels of silk
no matter how rough it hangs on those that receive.

tears of relief.

you aren't crying because they left. your tears are quiet
sighs of relief. welcome to your new life. a better life.

palace not a playground.

you are a palace. not a playground.
and you need to know that this place.
this time. this existence. this universe.
would not be the same without the
good energy you gift us. your dawn
is the sweetest sunrise.

soulaway.

you're giving way too much of yourself
to people who don't deserve it.

not putting you first.

their biggest mistake.

choose yourself more often.

you can't do everything
and be everything for everyone.
choose yourself more often.

your wings have always been ready.

your wings have always been ready. soar high. soar far. promise yourself to fly even when the sky looks like it's falling.

some people can't see angels.

dear beautiful soul.
nothing is wrong with you.
some people can't see angels.

stand out.

you were not made
to fit in.
you were made
to stand out.

universe in a star.

you are not a star in the universe.
you are the entire universe in a star.

you are more powerful than you think you are.

you are more powerful than you think you are. but.
for some reason. you dim your light. stop doing that.

thirsty.

your love
is a language
many thirst for
but will never
taste.

longing.

you are the kind of soul
someone is looking for.
longing for. wild for.

dear giver.

your vulnerability makes you beautiful.

givers.

givers have the capacity to overextend. overshare. overcare. over-
kind. overfeel. they distribute energy that fills others and releases
love without question. without thought. humans that give are
miracles. fall in love with a giver and you'll always be watered.

for once.

for so long it has been about them.
now)for once(let it be about you.

your biggest challenge.

you biggest challenge is that you care too much about what other
people think. you apologize when they are in the wrong. you're
a good person and have every right to stop accommadating and
start being firm and care more about your sunlight.

antidote.

you are the slow down and the appreciation of life. a hit of you.
a dose of you. a taste of you is the inhaler. is the elixir. is the
antiode. the sun sets on your cue. the moon anxiously awaits for
you to show your face. there is a special groove that can never
be duplicated. and the chilliest thing about you is the coolness of
your wind. in how you don't think yourself as cure or as anything
special. just as you. and that undersells your splendor. in ways that
makes you ten times doper. ten times the jazziest breeze. the kind
of breeze that so many try to catch and get a second chance to
experience. over and over again. once of you is never enough.
the wind follows you. a gentle rush of you sends souls off of their
feet and they dare not come down for fear of never feeling that
feeling ever again. as quiet as it is kept, antidotes mostly are kept
low in demand so it causes frenzy and turmoil and drives people
wild. drives people to think you unobtainable. inaccessible. too
good to talk to. but this isn't you. you are warm and welcoming.
no pedastal could keep you from being one with the people. one
with the simple. one with the gentle. one with the regular. one
with those who take in the same oxygen. just because people see
you as magic doesn't mean you don't appear. your desire to act like
simply you because you are just you. unaware of the fireworks you
create in others.

give more.

give more when they say give less. give more when they say you give too much. give more when they take. give more until you have no more to give left. give more because that is who you are. don't dim anything about you. giving is a super power. for you, giver of the world, are all that is good and beautiful.

when the sun goes missing.

something is always off when you quit coming around.
that's what happens when the sun goes missing.

emotional requirements.

it's okay to require
emotional connection
emotional attraction
emotional understanding
emotional vulnerability
emotional courage.

the most amazing thing about you.

the most amazing thing about you is your heart.
you give too much.

the tragedy is that others don't.

overflooded with deep love.

whoever you pour into i bet they are overflooded with deep love.

giving yourself an audience.

clap loud enough so that all parts of you feel loved.

not everyone is meant to touch the ocean floor.

it's okay if you're too deep.
not everyone is meant to touch the ocean floor.

there you are.

there you are. looking. searching. seeking. trying to find answers.
a bit unsure about what certain things mean. what this means.
there you are. anxious. scared. terrified. but no no no you can't
dare show it. no no you must keep that at bay. there you are.
uncertain yet maintaining but tired of this game of putting on a
brave face. there you are. spiraling trying to catch some sort of
sense. there you are. finally. i understand.

watch as fire and paper and words become smoke.

write down all the terrible things they said to you. the words that
keep you up and make you think you're not good enough. get all
of it out of your system. every sound phrase and feeling. then burn
it. watch as fire and paper and words become smoke. you aren't
what they say you are. you are the fire they are so afraid of. you are
roaring flames that can't be contained.

some people are just cruel. and terrible. and have nothing better
to do but try and pass on their bitterness and the wars that are
going on inside them onto others. and they also see the greatness
in others and instead of supporting and rooting and learning and
congratulating they have no good words to say. they mock and
downplay and make you second guess your own beauty your own
brilliance your own fire. and so you stop and question and begin
to believe their rhetoric. their speech. their virus. even if you know
how incredible you are. you value them and their opinion and
want to be accepted and seen and loved so you do)like any big
hearted person does(you took their feedback as truth and turned
into further thorns in your side. but from the outside looking in
i'll tell you this: don't accept their bitter pills. don't listen to their
fragility. their insecurities. their sadness. you are more than good
enough more than worthy more than sensational. and one day
you'll realize this. you'll step into the fire that you already are.
you'll become this force to be reckoned with and be unstoppable.
no words formed against you will see the light of day.

.

blindspot.

you're attached to people unworthy of you.

you.

you are the details of love. the fine edges.
the rough angles. what's most impressive
is how humble your heart is. you are rare.

league of your own.

you aren't one to be collected. or admired just to be toyed with.
to experience you is too much for those way out of your league.

you. beautiful. are in a league of your own. the bouquet of you
is arranged in such a way that you can't even be pronounced
correctly. there is no name that adequately describes you. and
that's because even the most decorated scientist or academic hasn't
discovered your element. my how wow you are. i can't even seem
to locate a proper sentence to make sense. the audience you accept
tremble in your presence. who wouldn't bend the knee to royalty.
only those who can't recognize magic before them.

bravery.

maybe it's your willingness to continue and carry on
with the pain inside you. maybe that is bravery after all.

keep going. and feel all the feelings. keep going. and give yourself
permission to fall. keep going. it's not about moving on or forget-
ting or pretending to be okay. it's about connecting with yourself.
being honest with yourself. and taking care of all the emotions
that come up while you take each step each breath each moment.
that is bravery. the willingness to continue and carry on with the
pain inside you.

sun yourself.

you are a lot of things to a lot of people.
they may not have the words to tell you.
but they love you. you are their sunshine.

without you there is no sun. no warmth. no light. no energy.
without you there is nothing but staleness. your presence is felt in
big ways but when you're away they are just off. disjointed. all they
know is they need you but their words get in the way. so even if
they keep it close)how they feel(about you tightly to themselves
know they love you. extremely. just unsure how to say it. but
maybe their love is in the smallness of things. the subtlest of
things. but it can be hard if you need verification. need hints of
affirmation. overt loving action. but know this: the sun seeks
no attention. sun just shines. sun just is. sun creates light. sun
makes love. so when you're in the mirror seeing yourself blinding
yourself this is why. the sun doesn't need to see itself. to know how
vibrant and hot and beautiful and stunning and necessary and
needed and loved it is. so sun if you're reading this. be like the sun.
know you are loved. everyone needs you. you mean a lot and are a
lot of things to a lot of people. so shine on. sun yourself love.
sun yourself love.

masumiya.

your impact may never be known to you. it may just sit in the
hearts of those who wouldn't be the same without you.

someone is truly thankful for you. they say it in their prayers. in
their affirmations. they write you down in their gratitude journals.
they speak your name in random heartbeats. they think of you
often. you make parties better and gifts are more meaningful
because you bought them. you made them. you touched them.
your thoughtful handwritten notes are supreme gestures of love.
and in some way you transfer an abundance of goodness that is
contagious. and when you smile)that smile(people smile back.
not in the that's the thing to do but because the chemistry inside
them responds to your gentle reminders of kindness. oh you.
beloved you. your impact may never be known to you but this big
big place is grandeur because of you. you are the hummingbird
and the flower. a sweet sweet soul. i love you. i love you. i love you.

for shoko.

you drown oceans.

you drown oceans.
you sink seas.
you level mountains.
you erupt volcanos.
you really are magic.

there there.

somehow you have this way of making hardship and bad days and sad times and stressful moments feel like happy passings. surmountable obstacles. rainbows in the clouds.

not sure how you do it. but you do. you find the positive in all things that have no business in what is gloom. but that's just you. your approach to life. the optimist. the greatest good.

that's needed. you are needed. in all the ways people need some-one. you are there. there there. there when no one expects it. there like you'd be there for yourself. because you know what it's like when no one is there. when no one shows up.

so to you. the one who shows. the one who is there. the one who would do anything for anyone. you are a gaze that resembles living dreams. a blissful ray upriver. what a muse you are. what a muse you are.

wasteland.

when you step across people that think they have nothing going
for them. people that have given up all hope. given up entirely. you
don't let them slide. and you don't make them feel shame or make
them do anything in particular. you just are who you are. and by
being you they miraculously become inspired. but this is not by
mistake or by pressure or by you making them change. you incite
in people a desire to try. to try. to try. to start again. to lift and do
for themselves what others have tried for so long to get them to
do. you see people guilt trip people all the time. and they are quick
to give up and throw them away. but you don't treat people like
wastelands. they are blank canvases worthy of new ink new acrylic
new brushes new water new purpose. and you do that for them.
not in the doing things for them. but the hopeful love and overall
genuine nature and spirit of you that you bestow upon them. how
bitter they have been treated left in the cold wanting warmth and
shelter and a love that understands. and there are you accepting
and listening and not fixing to fix but being to human being.
sad to say how rare. but there is you sending second chance chills
to those that need just a pick me up. you don't put them down or
make them feel worse. you affirm their state and ask what support
they may need. you aren't there to save or seek validation. you find
yourself in spaces with souls who need to be heard. need to be
witnessed. your big heart and desire makes all the difference.
by being you you are such a revolutionary act.

in a crowd of a thousand souls.

in a crowd of a thousand souls
there you are in your own world
head in technicolor clouds
rest of body grooving
to your own beat and rhythm
in a crowd of a thousand souls
you sometimes feel abandoned
lost in the swell of strangers
who once were close friends
you've grown but tried so hard
to fit in with people unmeant
in a crowd of a thousand souls
everyone searches for you
for someone like you
the you that doesn't care
the you that sets the tone
the you that dreams are made of
in a crowd of a thousand souls
your walk feels like a dance
your talk sounds like pure harmony
your energy breathmaking
your heart lifeguarding
in a crowd of a thousand souls
you just want to be left alone
blending in to escape for a time
to experience what it may be like
to flow with the current
rather than crashing against it.

nonchalant.

some things bother you and get under your skin. but you are
so in tune with your surroundings that there exists in you such an
unbothered nature. not that you shrug things off or nothing hits
you and makes you feel a certain way but on the whole you don't
let the small stuff take you off your game. maybe it's a shell or a
covering that can't be penetrated so easily but a nonchalant energy
rides alongside you. keeps you in stride. often times our lives bring
forth many obstacles presented as opportunities sent to get in the
way. as test to really see what you are made of. if you will quit. if
you will revert back to habits that no longer served you. but in a
matter of short pauses you're collected. calm. even if your nerves
shock your system pleading for you to act out of character and
flee. this bothers people who intentionally poke you. they want
to unhinge your aims and delay your greatness. and you see right
through. you see right through.

you flourish.

you don't age. you flourish. time shows all the abundance and all of the growth and all of the rainy days that felt like storms. inside you is an unlimited element. powers that exceed powers. took you a while to learn how to master it but with great magic comes great responsibility. to harness. to figure. to test and test and test. to see what you can do without being told to remove that part of you.

following the sun.

sun doesn't need space. it is space. it is its own entity. and no
matter how far away you get from it, it is always there. roaming.
pulsing. gathering. brightening. and when you think you are free
of it, the sun sits on your shoulder. breathing down your spine.
you are the sunniest. the highest. the divinist. the fullest. the most
coveted. sun. breaking from you is a break from universe and even
the furthest planet is closest to you. so when they run run run
away don't take offense. some can't stand in the light. some can't
breathe in the heat. and then there are those who need you
extremely. to survive to thrive to go on to love to understand to
find meaning. and then there is you. dear sun. stilling. and being.
souls can't but help to follow you. they can't help but follow you.

springtime.

when springtime comes you've already been warm. your leaves and your flowers already sprouted. your hibernation is during this time. when others gradually peak. you are in season every single day. vibrant and inspirational. springtime is your holiday. your celebration. your honoring period. it is this window between cold and hot that the world blooms for you.

another dimension.

you want to feel something. something different.
something you've never felt. something real.
something like you. someone like you.

tempest.

some find comfort
after the storm
but you find comfort
in the tempest
where most
seek shelter
you go
where
the
winds
take
you.

sinner.

a sinner is just a soul who missed the target. who stepped off
the beaten path to find their own way through instead of going
around. they tell you that only sinners go below below instead of
above above. but you make room for everyone who just asks to be
forgiven for not hitting the mark. but you're just like them. making
your way. making mistakes. making do. figuring out what is right.
navigating what feels true. in truth there are no sinners. just souls
looking for light. looking to wander more. looking for others
who've been told they are broken.

hurricane.

sometimes what you fear the most
is what you need. and many have feared you.
the few who have expressed interest have said
they could withstand your pouring your rain
your torrential personality. but they didn't know
that you were a hurricane. but you warned them.
you warned them. you told them advised them
to prepare for all the seasons in a flame.
and when you hit they were nowhere
to be found. washed away.

fire eyes.

you need someone
who can see
the fire
in your eyes.
someone
not looking
to extinguish
your flame
someone
looking
to set
themselves
on fire
as
well.

trumpet trumpet.

can you hear it.
the trumpet
playing
solo
cutting
cutting
cutting
against
orchestra
against
bass
against
drum
signaling
to your
brass
love
it's welcome
it's welcome
can you hear it.
right there
right
there.

encouraging you still.

heaven knows what you have been through. many times over.
this one hurt the deepest. stung strongest. leaving you longing.
longing. longing. with an almost unbearable ache. sometimes no
matter the answer or response or reasons tried to be given don't
make a difference. won't take the dent out. won't justify. but you
carry on. you carry them. with you. wherever you are. wherever
you go. they are there. they are there. holding you up. nudging you
forward. and they are there in your quietude. when you can't
contain your emotions. and you get flanked and let go. they are
there by you. holding space with you. they've become so much
more than they were before. and as hard as it is to grasp this new
relationship. this new experience. this teaches you how to love
again. how to reach and reach and reach and reach and reach and
re-discover the world. you are reminded that they are not gone.
they are always here. right here. right now. saying something to
your soul. you can feel it hit you as you smile. they sit in every
memory. they are forever around. you just can't forget. although
they would never let you. but you can never forget to tell all their
stories out loud and in whispers. the one who taught you how to
be how to love. the one who encouraged you is enouraging you
still.

discover your light.

when you discover your light
it will be where it has always been
inside you
where most people look last.
that is where you'll find love.

when they see you.

you are on everybody's list of favorite people. this is because you
don't conform. you're just you. authentic. refreshing. real. and
everyone loves you. everyone. everyone. when you're not somewhere they ask where you are if you are coming. why you aren't
there. when you can't make it people get sad because the entire
experience is just off. different. just not the same. everybody wants
to be your friend. and this is shocking to you. people confide in
you. they tell you things they don't tell their person person. you
are the first they want to call and the first they want to hug. you're
unlike anyone because you're just you. to the fullest. and that is
refreshing. so damn refreshing. like new air new life new
beginnings. when they see you they flock to you. like mirage in
a desert. you seem unreal but you are. in amazement they know
how lucky they are to know you. you're like their very own star.
when they see you they wish upon you. even when you aren't
there there in person. they send up thoughts in hopes you will see
them and catch their words. when they see you they stand at
attention and wonder in awe what you'll do next. but when
they see you you wish they wouldn't. wouldn't make a big deal.
wouldn't give you attention. wouldn't treat you any different. but
your humility is endearing. they see you in what they want in
themselves. everyone has someone they look to for guidance. for
motivation. for encouragement. and you are that. all of that and
more. when they see you they see potential of how they could be.
because you are a mirror. they see their own reflection in you.

crash and crumble.

trust people fully because that is who you are. how you are. don't wall up in spite. it will ruin you. so trust with all your might. your trust is a boost to the system for without your unconditional spirit the universe shall crash and crumble.

where you happen to burst alive.

you love to fly. airplanes remind you of your own outsretched wings. sitting and staring from your window seat your imagination takes you away into the clouds cutting through where sky blends with blues and purple swirls. you are now the pilot. jet setting and gliding where your heart is most happy. this is clarity. a deep sigh high above the stratosphere where you happen to burst alive.

up close you are proof.

up close you are proof that love is everlasting. that love is more than feeling more than gravity itself. that love is a filled in color in your image. in how you approach. in how you fulfill dreams. you are the shooting dust a star leaves after it takes off and lingers. lingers. lingers. and lands just above ground like a fresh paused moment no one wants to ever end. you spill with not even a care of how you fall. this wasn't always the case. this took many trials. many mishaps. many experiences of wishing you could take back what you gave in order to avoid further pain. but those were exhausting times. and now you've accepted the not being understood. and the parts of you so many robbed from you. you are no longer unhindered by perception. it will always be their misperception that plagues them. not you. not you. no more. you took yourself back and became recklessly brave. where you used to avoid wrecks for fear of the mess and now you run into the fire because you know you are made of fire. and you used to be too far away from yourself but now you are up close to yourself. proof to yourself that just because someone wants to keep you from shin-ing doesn't actually keep you from shining. it makes you brighter. so much brighter. and rather than feel sorry for those who wish you dim you send them bright vibes back. there is no room in you to wish darkness on anyone. you are love before love was even a word and before love was even spoken and before love had its own language. you are. and that is profound.

tiger growling for the roam.

there is a tiger in you. still. at the ready. growling for the roam.
waiting for something. waiting for something. you don't just show
this side of you. you are this side of you. but you patiently let it
drip from you rather than release it all at once. your determination to achieve what you set out to accomplish is intimidating but
only because your fierceness pushes others to push themselves
and you set the bar so high. and nothing you can do will ever
lower or change that. nothing. so don't even try. your mediocre is
a master level. average is outstanding. your patience can feel a bit
aggressive because there is an assumption that you want perfect.
but you don't want perfect. you want authentic. you want raw. you
want heart. and without those things you don't want any part. this
tiger in you is dormant yet present. always rumbling under your
ribcage. indulging in your third eye and glowing from within. you
may be unpredictable but your unpredictability and willpower and
personal strength is inspiring. you send shockwaves against any
fears and doubts and obstructions that try and deter and come
near. you teach others how to survive just by learning yourself
how to overcome what tries to chain you down.

pour. spill. give.

pour. spill. give.
no matter
no matter
and in the wake of
judgement and
ridicule and
pressure to
unbecome
stick to
your bones
your stars
your deepest inner
and
always
always
always
share
who you are
lift your voice
even if it trembles.

soft.

so much desire to be hard and rough and rock and solid and less emphasis on the fluid and the wave and the slow and the soft. the ability to be pure emptiness and still be quite full. quite complete. in silence. in solitude. in quiet corners of the mind and the finding of unfiltered peace. a sacred place. a state of being. that withstands and withholds. that takes in grenades and turns them into powder. there is so much power in your softness. in your ability to turn rapids into shallow waters. that takes strength. to literally re-direct and absorb without turning into that which is built to downpour and pounce and shatter and replace with all the parts it hits you with. to turn you into who you were never meant to be. you can't help but take on some of what they throw at you because you find good even if there is no good to be had. but you get it. you get it. and you show it. you share it. even if they can't see it. dark water too has light. and you survived their trial. survived their tsunami. survived their anguish and still so still. intact. not because you were hard or rock or solid but because you remained soft.

the well.

you go out of your way to help others. as if you hear their cry
before the cry itself begins. your senses pick up on who needs
to be called. who needs to be checked in on. who needs a care
package. a love package. a just because handwritten note slipped
somewhere they will see and remember someone is thinking of
them. you are a nurturer. a caregiver. it doesn't feel like you go out
of your way because your way is always towards them. towards
someone. towards your purpose. if a struggle is occuring you are
one moment away from being the flowers and the listener and the
advisor and the friend and the container. you are the well. one that
you both spill out of and into. a soul that isn't there to fix or patch
or rectify but to be present and provide what support may be
needed. and of course you wonder if people would do this for you.
some do. but sometimes not the ones you really want to be there.
and that is hard on you. but a well can't dictate who draws from it.
but a well can determine how much water gets pulled from it. and
those buckets who keep coming down coming down you notice
the gratitude. and the shift in energy when they sip from you.
although you want to sometimes siphon and cut off and stop alto-
gether but when you do this your own essence is thrown off. not
the same. you are not yourself. and those who share space with
you can tell. and they are impacted. not because they aren't able
to get into your well but because your well has run dry. don't dam
yourself. don't dam yourself. don't dam yourself. putting yourself
before others is not a weakness it is wonderful strength. gifted to
you to give. when you drain yourself the entire natural world gets
drained too. because you're connected. spiritually. emotionally.
energetically. by giving you get so much back because the universe
speaks your name. honors every bit of your being. what a fine
giver you are. what a gem you are. what a remarkable soul you are.

you're not broken you're unfinished.

a vile that looks fragile doesn't make it delicate. because it is see-
through doesn't mean it isn't made with reinforced steel.
you quake and have fault lines and have your own tipping point.
your own threshold of when to say enough is enough. inside you
there is some unresolved stuff that bubbles up every now and
then. and most often you ignore it and other times it causes you to
lose sleep. you want to move on and dig out what haunts you away
far away so you can have days that don't gnaw at you. days that
don't make you think that you are the root of the problem. days
that make you think you are broken. but you're not broken you're
unfinished. you have stories that make many flinch. but you are
not the sum of your hurt and pain. your testimony is a story that's
still being written. and while how you feel is valid and how you
want so bad to not feel down this is part of the journey. this part
is meant to turn you into gold. but you have to change the voice in
your head and you have to tell yourself over and over that this will
pass. so you have to talk back. you have to claw back. you need to
sit and listen to every ounce of feeling and every sound and every
word that these wounds are trying to say and pull them out. and
keep pulling. until every piece has had its peace. and give it peace
by telling it peace. and soon all of it will fade and this will be in
your rearview. remember. no part of you is broken. not at all.
you are simply unfinished. your body your mind your soul your
heart your elements your footprints your aura your everything
is beautiful. your everything is beautiful. your everything is beautiful. and although things seem to not be going your way right
now or you have a little more doubt than you have confidence you
need to know you're not alone. you're not alone. you're not alone.
face the storm. head on. cry out. tell it to try and break you but
refuse to back down. all that fight in you. you bloom as you fight.

what your own waters heal like.

the plant doesn't care where it gets rain from so long as any rain comes. but rain from you isn't just any type of rain. it comes from the bottom of a never ending source. a source of tranquility and harmony. substance and nourishment. you have a built-in ability to tap into your self. and create the love and become the love that you need. for yourself. for others. but it isn't selfish to do this for you. to be what you are to others exclusively for you. and when you do decide to spend some time some energy some money some moments just with you i know you feel guilty. you think it unnecessary but going inward and serving your needs is funda-mental. it is how you remain in touch with who you are without losing yourself. because you matter, too. you are essential, too. rain isn't just for you it is you. and before you can fall and fall and fall and fall into and on anyone else you need to know what your own waters taste like. what your own waters heal like. what your own powers power like. be proud of yourself. take this time to think about how far you have come not in the number of souls you have served but in the countless breaths you have breathed yourself. autopilot can run you ragged because your normal speed is forever at a five but slow down. slow down. slow. down. and honor yourself. bask in your own sun. in your own stars. in your own moon. in your own earth. in your own way. my how people envy you. they wish you could see you how they see you. but even as you resist slowing down and pouring in you also miss the lights in front of you. can you see them. the way people just turn on and glow and shift and change right before your eyes. thank you may not leave their mouths but deep gratitude fills their souls. take this with you next time you break and relax and halt your mind. rub this on your heart. you don't hear it often but you should. you are the most beautiful giver. the most beautiful giver.